PEYTON & PAIGE

JUDE E. MCNAMARA

CONTENTS

COPYRIGHT

Author Contact

Website: www.judeemcnamara.com

Email: jude@judeemcnamara.com

Facebook: Jude E. McNamara

Twitter: @judeemcnamara

Instagram: iamtwojudes

Two Judes Publishing (A division of Two Judes Media Group)

668 Stony Hill Road Suite 339

Yardley, Pennsylvania 190687

ISBN: 978-1-7371778-0-7 (ebook)

ISBN: 978-1-7371778-1–4 (print)

ACKNOWLEDGMENTS

I wish to thank my core group of talented beta readers—Nicole Arnold, Jeanine Hillesland, Donna Nelson and Shonta Young. Your feedback was invaluable, motivating me to press forward until I got the story right. I'm blessed to have you behind me in this writing journey. I am forever grateful.

Shout out to my writing coach, Audrey Hughey at *Author Transformation Alliance*. You remain my "go-to" person for all things story.

To my readers around the globe: Thank you purchasing my novels, sharing my stories on your blogs and with your book clubs. You have welcomed me into your world and helped to make my dreams possible.

DEDICATION

To Louise and James. Know that when I fall, I fall looking up.
You are forever my ribbons in the sky.

SYNOPSIS

PEYTON & PAIGE

Peyton

White-collar crime is my specialty. But you couldn't tell it by the female sitting across the conference room table from me. She's one red line away from robbing my family of its generational wealth, taking my heart with her. Foolish me for stepping out of my lane to help my brother get hitched and protect what's both his and mine. I'm the last person that should be here. Not because I'm not good at what I do. But because she wants to break my balls and all I want to do is to give them to her on a silver platter.

Paige

My job doesn't normally make me anxious. Today is different. The legal shark extraordinaire is in the room. Yes, that guy. A *heated* battle is his signature form of foreplay. But I have a game plan of my own. A game I plan to win and run him straight off the rails, right into my crosshairs. Got your popcorn out?

CHAPTER ONE

I take one last pull on my cigarette blowing smoke through my nose, contorting my mouth in the shape of an O, making smoke rings in the air for kicks. A gust of wind blows through the air causing my brown curly hair to sweep across my right eye. It's the first day of spring, but you'd hardly know it by the wind chill in the air. I grab the lapels of my tan trench coat, flipping the collar up for warmth. I flick the butt end of my cigarette on the concrete sidewalk, taking the tip of my black patent Louboutin to crush the flame out. Once again, my habit of stress smoking arises like clockwork whenever I'm forced to go up against him. It's the only time my job as an attorney makes me antsy.

He knows he's a turn on. He racks my nerves causing me to lose my focus. I can see his arrogant drop-dead handsome face, giving me that shit grin. The one where he undresses me with his smoldering emerald green eyes. It's his tell that he wants me and that he's looking forward to the battle. We both know a contentious battle is his form of foreplay. A battle where we take turns seeing which one of us is leaving with the pot of gold. Today my money is on me. *I'm in it to win it*, I counsel myself.

My phone pings for the third time reminding me that I need to head inside to let the games begin. I don't answer the text. I know who it is and once again I make the choice to ignore it. The man on the phone is not my priority at this moment.

I proceed through the revolving doors that are turning automatically without my touch. I feel my anxiety level elevate as I mentally will this damn slow-moving door to open. It cracks slightly ajar. I scamper to the bank of elevators towards the half-opened elevator door that is about to close.

"Hold that door please," I shout as I pick up my pace, my stilettos clacking across the polished grey marble floor. An older, grey-haired man in a bespoke suit removes his fedora and stops the half-opened elevator door from closing. I step inside. I breathe heavily but still I mind my manners and give him a huge smile. He gives me a sly wink I know I've seen before.

"Thank you for holding the door for me," I puff breathily.

Yes, my mother, bless her heart, is big on social graces. The old man nods at me.

My heart rate begins to slow. I remind myself once again to commit to quitting my need for a stress cigarette. I reach inside my tote, grabbing the tic-tacs, tossing a trio of winter-green pellets in my mouth to conceal my guilty stress pleasure.

"Thirty please."

"I happen to be going to that same floor too, beautiful. Our lucky day, no?"

"The luck of the Irish," I quip back, recalling that today is St. Patrick's Day.

The old man grins wide at me. I smile as he pushes the

white glowing button marked thirty. His flashy diamond pinkie ring catches my attention. I steal a glance at him out the corner of my eye. He's every bit of eighty years old. Well dressed. Silver-white hair. Manicured hands. His light grey shark-skinned silk suit has to have cost a small fortune. Yup, he's old money. He'd be my first pick to pose on the cover of a Brooks Brothers catalog, senior edition. Everything about him makes it obvious that he's a member of the Top of the Thirty Club, the private, members-only restaurant on the thirtieth floor.

"You're welcome to join me and my companion for a cocktail," he drools while sporting a devilish grin with a twinkle in his eye. "Such a coincidence we're going to the same floor."

He looks at me as if I'm the afternoon delight. I take a few steps to my left to put some personal space between us. The old man tugs on the shirt cuffs of his monogrammed shirt. The initials W.M. are embroidered in blue thread on his cuffs. I look at him side-eyed. Suddenly, I'm feeling like the old coot is on the hunt and I'm the prey.

"There are no coincidences," I answer back, my arched eyebrow raised. "But I tend to think three's a crowd. Thank you anyway."

"Well, that depends," he chuckles. "Threesomes can be a lot of fun in my experience."

Is the old man propositioning me, or am I misinterpreting him? While I'm thankful the old man has held the elevator for me, it's headed thirty floors up. God knows I may not survive a chitchat with a dirty old rich fuck in the elevator of Philadelphia's One Liberty Place.

Imagine it. I can see the *Page Six* article now. *Paige Holland, renowned attorney to Philadelphia's own prominent list of who's who, and daughter of the eminent fashion*

African-American designer Amos Holland, caught in a three-some snare with an eighty-year-old silver fox old-money geezer as she ascends to the top floor conference room to join all those top legal eagle money guns pointed at each other.

Yes, I was here to protect all those riches belonging to my bestie Lexi Wang. Yes, *the* Lexi Wang. Philadelphia's own Thirty Over Thirty, Korean news anchor, heiress princess to the Wang media magnate family fortune, whose future marriage to attorney and managing partner with the Morrone Group, LLC and now a U.S Senatorial candidate, Kelsey Morrone, is *the* talk of the town.

The elevator button dings as we reach the thirtieth floor, forcing me to focus on the reason I am here—to negotiate the pre-nuptial agreement for Lexi.

A petite, white-haired, well-dressed lady wearing a Tiffany blue Chanel suit, white gloves in hand, and holding Tory Burch's latest alligator handbag is standing in front of the elevator doors. She waits patiently as the old man steps to the side holding the elevator door open for me. He tips his hat. Once I step out, the old man flashes his cheeky grin at her as she hooks her arm inside of his. He bends down and kisses her cheek, but not before he turns to wink at me as she leads him down the long hallway, turning to the right, heading to the Top of the Thirty Club. It all makes sense. Truman Capote with his Lee Radziwill. No way he could ever think I'd be in a throuple with that sweet little loving couple. But I have to admit, I admire the old man's confidence.

I give the old geezer a quick wink and a sly grin. I check my phone text that is pinging again. The older couple departs down the long hallway to the right, and I turn to the left. It's showtime. But first I must deal with the one man who shakes my world and moves mountains in this town. He thinks I'm the one who moves his world, but really, he moves mine.

My text message alert buzzes again.

SHAKER: You're late!

I give myself a mental jiggle, deciding whether to answer him or not. *God, the man has guts*! He knows I'm on an important mission today. This is not the time to bug me. Nevertheless, I decide to put him out of his misery and rest his mind at ease.

MOVER: I promise I will talk to you later. Lexi needs me today.

SHAKER: I need you. And, I have something special planned for tonight.

MOVER: Patience. I'm gonna kick ass and take names for Lexi. So fair warning. I'll be in a good mood this evening coming off my win. I'll be coming in hot, both barrels loaded AF. You should concentrate on being ready for me. You're MY special.

SHAKER: Such a tease baby. I love it when you talk dirty to me.

MOVER: Does this mean if I shoot your dog, you're gonna kill my kitty cat?

SHAKER: Plan on it sweetheart. Me and my big dog will be waiting for you.

MOVER: Meow, bad boy.

I wipe the grin he can't see off my face, swapping it for my poker face. I close my phone, tucking it inside my quilted black leather tote bag. I focus back on the matter at hand. The man in the next room will be looking for his own takedown this afternoon. This negotiation would be smooth sailing but for the shitstorm that will be waiting for me across the conference room table. A shitstorm named Peyton Morrone. Yes. That Peyton Morrone. Legal shark extraordinaire. The best in the business. Well versed in the art of legal shenanigans, and today's Mister Pain-in-My-Ass.

Peyton Morrone, Italian-American, suave, intellectually brilliant. A handsome heartthrob known for garnering the attention of every woman that graces his path. He's their flame and they are the wannabe moths. His reputation for turning ladies' heads precedes him. But who could blame them? He's practically irresistible. Whenever I go up against him as opposing counsel, I have to be extra diligent to maintain my composure so as not to get caught in his web. He uses every asset in his tool box of seductive weaponry. He never fails to use his panty-dropping, sexy-as-fuck smile to give himself the competitive edge. He loves winning as much as I do, which makes us evenly matched. And that is saying something, because I hate to lose. And I have a stellar winning streak to prove it.

If it weren't for the heated stares he's given me in some of our more contentious courtroom battles causing me to lose my grip, I would think he was all hat and no cattle. But I know better. He's got the guns to back up that legal eagle brain. He's a serious challenger. One that I welcome taking a swing at and cracking his armor. Even if it's outside the courtroom for a mere contract negotiation like the one I'll be battling with him today.

This day, however, all the gloves are off. I'm not forced to share a courtroom on opposite sides with a judge between us to regulate our free-for-all. Game on to that handsome face. I shall not be deterred by his renowned allure. I intend to see that Lexi enters into her marriage financially secure and laying claim to everything she deserves while keeping all that is hers. I will take no prisoners for my bestie. Girl Power matters, right? So what that he has a few years of experience on me. I'm well trained by the best legal mind in town. I can do this.

I push open the heavy oak door leading to the conference room reserved for our meeting. The mahogany conference table is set with a tray of water glasses, and crystal pitchers filled with water. Stacks of yellow legal pads and bunches of loose black ballpoint pens sit in a huge pile next to the pads. Rays of afternoon sunlight peek through the wall of windows on the left side of the room that overlooks the city. Lexi is standing near the credenza. It's lined with water bottles in a neat row with three-tiered stands filled with assorted fruits and pastries. Lexi is hovering over the long table with a pimento cheese finger sandwich in her hand, cooing at Kelsey, her thirty-two-year-old soulmate, fiancé and the love of her life.

She's taken the day off, and has shed her professional journalistic armor. Today she's not suffering from a failure to conform at thirty-one. She's wearing a neon yellow, pink, and black polka dot midriff top, gold choker, with a white blouse tied at the waist. She's rocking a short denim mini skirt with white patent heels. She looks like a high-end boho chic Kimora Lee Simmons version of a fan girl at a BTS concert. No need for me to reign her in because however she manages to do it, she's pulled the rich K-pop rocker fan girl image off flawlessly. So, I silence my inner fashion critic, a habit that is a by-product of growing up with a famous fashion designer father.

Her thick long black curls are pulled neat in a high pony-tail, with a loose tendril falling down the side of her face, her diamond hoops sparkling in the partly cloudy sunlight peeking through the wall of glass windows. Lexi mumbles some Korean words at Kelsey that sound sexy with a sprinkle of dirty in between. I have no idea what she is saying, but I can tell by the look on Kelsey's face that he's madly turned on. She's been teaching him her language. I'm pretty sure he knows all the dirty words she's saying to him. I inwardly chuckle to myself. At the end of the day, I'm ecstatic that she has found her person.

A smile creeps on my face when I think about my own person, who at thirty-five has mentored me through law school. Now that I am twenty-eight, my legal skills are almost as keen as his own. But I cut that memory short, immediately putting my poker face on as I eyeball the pitbull in the corner of the room, who is busy twisting the cap off of a Pellegrino and taking a huge gulp. His inky black hair is combed neatly back with a side part. A wayward strand falls slightly down on his forehead. His trimmed beard frames his chiseled jaw. His mustache lines kissable lips that he licks while sliding his Tom Ford's down the bridge of his nose. He rests them on top of his head. He ogles at me with his award-winning panty-dropping stare so heated it un-nerves me. His first line of attack. I turn my attention away from him so as not to get distracted. I focus on the loving couple across the room who are knee deep in pre-marital bliss.

"You two should get a room," I say to Lexi as I take my tan trench jacket off and sling it and my tote bag in the empty high-back leather side chair closest to me. I walk towards her, putting my arms out to hug Lexi.

"Paige," Lexi squeals. She sees me, moving towards me to embrace my open arms with a big hug.

"Peyton was just telling Kelsey and me that we should all go to Paddy's afterwards to drink green shots of Irish whiskey. You know, to celebrate after we sign all these contracts."

She waves her hand across the stack of legal pads in front of us.

"We should get this business over quick. You know how much I hate talking about money," Lexi says, squishing her nose up in a frown. "Right, honey?" she nods at Kelsey's direction.

"Yeah, babycakes," Kelsey co-signs. "Let's get this over so we can all go do some shots. What do you think, brother?" Kelsey nods at Peyton. "What do you say you have Jackie close the office up early. It's Friday on St. Paddy's day. Time to kick back."

"I already gave Jackie and the staff the rest of the afternoon off," Peyton sighs.

I hear his exhale.

"I predicted the meeting would be long. I knew we wouldn't be returning."

Peyton and Kelsey are partners in The Morrone Group, a family-owned law firm located on the eighteenth floor of this very building. Jackie, the firm's administrator, is the one woman in the office that hasn't been driven off by Peyton's anal-retentive ways.

"Ah, I don't know," I mumble pulling my binder out of my tote bag, organizing my notes in front of me. This was not the time to get distracted with talks of whiskey shots.

"It'll be fun," Lexi coos. "It's the start of March Madness, remember?"

"Oh yeah, Peyton, Villanova is playing tonight," Kelsey adds.

Peyton and Kelsey high-five each other, exchanging words in Italian and laughing, leaving Lexi and I out of their little private joke.

I throw daggers at the both of them, thinking this can't happen. I have plans tonight. If I survive this negotiation with

Mr. Hot and Bothered, my kitty-cat's gonna need some serious attention. Peyton runs his finger through his silky hair, his Adam's apple bobbing. He takes another gulp of water, glancing at me through long lashes, his gaze raking my body. His smile is seductive. I swear the man is a certifiable flirt. *Don't look at him. Don't look at him. Don't look at him.*

I peer down at my notes, swallowing hard before my eyes stray to him. We lock eyes. I squint at him, blowing out a heavy breath, daring him to turn this picture into a double date because I know what's coming next out of those delicious lips.

"Yeah, Paige. I'm all in for some whiskey shots this Friday afternoon," Peyton says, flashing his breathtaking smile. His eyes soften and he winks, testing my need for control.

Holy fuck. *Why aren't I surprised, Mr. Drop Dead Gorgeous?*

He's baiting me. He thinks if I agree to go for shots later that I'll put my guard down and behave as if we're one happy family, making me forget why I'm here.

"Fine," I snap, realizing I'm outnumbered. Far be it for me to be the one to steal Lexi's joy. But I refuse to be outgunned. Peyton's going to need those shots when I get done with him.

"Good, it's settled then," Lexi says, rubbing her hands together, her five-carat, pear-shaped diamond glittering in the sunlight coming through the window.

I glance down at my own tan-lined ring finger. He stares incredulously at me, tugging on his leather bracelet that is sliding out from the cuff of his crisp white shirt. His expression and mood revealing a flash of defiance.

"Let's get this show on the road. I need this meeting over. I'm overdue for some fun and games."

I give her a wide grin and pat her on the shoulder. She flashes her come-hither grin at Kelsey. Her secret weapon. Gets him every time. I give thought to the fact I could use a few weapons of my own. A machete perhaps, to take him down a few notches. I raise my head and flash a huge grin his way.

"No worries," I say, glaring at Peyton, challenging him.

He shifts in his seat.

"We got this, Lexi."

"Do you?" Peyton utters with a smoldering smirk that sends a flight of butterflies fluttering throughout my stomach.

I open my file.

"Here, I have something for the both of you."

I slide Peyton a copy of Lexi's financial statements and a list of her marital expectations for his and Kelsey's review. I beam sweetly. Lexi is busy playing *Words with Friends* on her phone as if she doesn't have a care in the world. She really doesn't. We discussed her list of prenup requests a week ago. We're ready.

"Guys, take a few minutes to review these documents." Kelsey nods in acknowledgment. Peyton is nonresponsive, not finding his words, though he grabs the documents and slides the second copy in Kelsey's direction.

"Please excuse me. I need to run to the ladies' room." I nod at the both of them.

Lexi waves her hand at me dismissively, her focus never leaving her word game. She's bored with all matters regarding money. She's heir to so many millions from her family it's like she treats money as an annoyance. It's merely a means to an end for her. I figure Peyton is similarly minded as he, too, is in line for generational wealth.

Peyton and Kelsey both rise as I move out of my chair and head out the conference room. I walk into the nearby ladies' room, pulling my phone out of my jacket pocket, my thumbs working the text quickly. There's a dangerous and mystifying man I need to subdue first if I plan to trot off with this raucous group to Paddy's. Whiskey shots at Paddy's could make for a long night. I send a text.

Mover: Sorry, but I'm going to be a later than expected. Change of plans with Lexi and her boo. I have somewhere else I need to be.

Shaker: Need to be? Or want to be?

Mover: Both. I have wants. And I have needs.

Shaker: I need to be where you are. If you have needs, I want to be the one to take care of them.

Mover: Sounds promising.

Shaker: I'm your man then. The keeper of promises.

I hit the red slider shutting my phone off. I catch a glimpse of myself in the bathroom mirror, giving myself a cheesy grin like I've won the cover of *Essence* magazine. I smooth off the front of my navy pin-striped pencil skirt with my hand, tucking my silk, silver, pearl-buttoned blouse neatly inside the waist band. I tuck my phone inside the pocket of my matching single-breasted jacket. I pull out the tiny pot of Candy Baby gloss out of my other pocket and dab my lips softly, pressing them together as I check myself out in the mirror. All this talk about wants, needs, promises, coupled with whiskey shots on the horizon has me needing to check and double check everything including my appearance. I fight off the urge to stress smoke, and splash some sprinkles of cold water on my neck and in the V of my breast to cool myself down.

This is not how this afternoon was supposed to go. A handsome dangerous man across the conference room table in front of me is on the hunt and a smoking hot, sex-on-a-stick is working my phone.

I waltz back in the conference room unaware there is a black tornado swirling about me. I take my seat in front of the Italian stallion who is firing green daggers at me. I count to ten in my head. He's on the brink of shorting a fuse any second. I'm next to Lexi, who is immune to the sudden change in Peyton's mood. But his brooding demeanor is not lost on me. I close my manicured fingers together in front of me knowing he's digested the list of our demands.

"So, Mr. Morrone, let's say we get this prenup in place for our two lovebirds."

Peyton slams his palm on the table in front of me so hard it causes the water pitcher to bounce as beads of water skitter across the large mahogany table. Lexi flinches, raising her head from her word game. She gapes at Kelsey, who is ignoring Peyton's outburst, as he is still spastically flipping through the financials of the documents. I purse my lips, not surprised. His temper tantrum is predictable.

"Fuck, Paige! What the fuck? What are you exactly? A thief? A robber?"

I'm fist bumping myself inside. I have Peyton right where I want him. On the ropes and in my crosshairs. He's practically on fire trying to contain himself. He knows I'm coming in for the kill. *Poor baby. I know how you hate to lose.*

"Are you telling me if this marriage ends in divorce before five years are up, that Lexi gets fifty percent of Kelsey's shares in the Morrone Group? Have you lost your mind?" Peyton hisses. "Good God, woman."

"Ahh…yeah," I answer back, tickled pink that Peyton's in a state of frenzy.

"What's wrong, you think your boy can't last in a marriage five years, Peyton? He's running for the Senate. Bitches and hos will be swarming on him like pastry addicts racing to Dunkin' Donuts. Kelsey needs to have some skin in the game. He needs to be invested in this marriage," I snap back.

"Morrone Group is MY family's firm. It's a legacy of generations built on the back and sweat of Morrones. Not Lexi Wang."

I watch Peyton's facial expression as he snaps, his temper flaring, causing him to lose his edge as he mentally comes off the rails.

"Over my dead body, Paige," he barks with a defiant edge in his voice.

The thrill of victory is within my reach. I'm like an Olympian going for the gold. Or better yet, color me David beating down Goliath with a slingshot to the head.

Yeah, baby. Hit me with that sexy smile of yours once more. This is the part of that little foreplay of yours that I like best. I think I'm the one with the hard on. Give me what I want and give it to me now.

"Should I be taking that crack personal, Peyton?" Kelsey interjects, "I've worked hard to get where I am in the Morrone Group. It's not all your sweat in the game, dude. It's mine too. Motherfucker, I'm family."

It's not lost on me that Kelsey put a special emphasis on the word *family*. Lexi raises her eyebrows as if wondering what's coming next. All she needs is a tub of popcorn to watch the shitstorm I knew was coming.

"Lexi doesn't need Morrone shares. She's got more fucking money than sense," Peyton booms.

My eyes widen. Oh, this is so bad. He's hurling insults at my client? I will cut his left ball off for that slip of the tongue.

Yeah. I know where he could put better use of that tongue....Did I just think that?

"Tell me how you really feel, Peyton!" Lexi yelps. "For the record, I'm not stupid. Are you butt hurt that Kelsey is off the market and has to keep his joystick in his pants? Can't live vicariously through him anymore?" she huffs, giving both Peyton and Kelsey a murderous glare.

Surprising me, Kelsey rises to the occasion. *He's not looking too much like a beta, contrary to what Lexi thinks, going head-to-head with his alpha brother.*

"You take that back right now, Peyton," Kelsey snaps, rising to his feet, balling his fist, his reddened face turning towards Peyton with a commanding stand.

Perhaps Kelsey is on the brink of cutting off Peyton's left ball for me. I need my own tub of popcorn for the scene that is unfolding before me. I'm starting to even feel a little bit sorry for Peyton, but I know he can handle the rush of heat. I give off a murderous vibe as our gazes ping pong between the group.

Peyton rises with him, his six-foot-three frame matching Kelsey's six-foot-two. He smooths his crisp white shirt, running his hands down the front of it. He loosens the knot of his silk silver tie, placing a hand in the pocket of his grey charcoal pants. His expression has turned apologetic from the mere fact his balls are being caught in a vice of his own making.

I shake my head, disappointed in Peyton for taking a swipe at Lexi, but I know I need to snap the guys out of their testosterone stupor that has turned into a scene of whose balls are bigger. They are brothers. Family. I doubt they will come to physical blows, but there is a first time for everything so I won't lay bets that it couldn't happen. I cross my arms across my chest in disbelief of the scene playing out in front of me.

"Boys. Control yourselves. We're all frenemies here," I plead, chuckling to myself. *Now I've got jokes.*

"I'm not so sure who is friends with who at this point," Kelsey mutters.

Peyton growls at Kelsey.

"I'm on your team, Kelsey," Peyton elbows him in the ribs, admonishing him.

Kelsey takes a step back, murmuring curses under his breath. Agitated, he runs both hands through his dark smoky hair much like his brother does when he's annoyed. His broad chest expands as he takes a deep exhaling breath.

"Real talk, Peyton. You could have fooled me, insulting my fiancé like that."

The way I see it, Kelsey is team Lexi right now. *That's right, Peyton. My team.*

I snicker under my breath, aware that Peyton has momentarily lost his composure, something he rarely does. I have put a chink in his armor. The mere thought of it brings me great joy. *In it for the win, baby.*

Peyton looks guilty as sin, but he's aware I expected him to rein himself in and do the right thing even though I was sure Satan had taken possession of his good wits.

I give him the stink eye to prod him along. *Do the right thing, Peyton, or I'll launch another grenade at you.*

Peyton coughs, clearing his throat.

"Please accept my apology, Lexi. That behavior was beneath me. You are, in fact, a very bright woman. I know this because Kelsey is in love with you, and you're friends with Paige. Ms. Holland never ever surrounds herself with stupid," he says through gritted teeth. "Everyone in town knows that. Please accept my apology."

He's dropped the Paige and I'm Ms. Holland now. His dander is up. Winning.

Lexi nods in agreement, looking as if she feels a little sorry for Peyton.

I roll my eyes at Lexi. *Don't you dare feel sorry for him. He's a big dog. He can handle it.*

"I'm sorry, Kelsey, for my loss of decorum. Please forgive me," Peyton mutters shamefully. "Lexi's a great catch and you're lucky to have her. I don't know what came over me."

I know what came over you. I came over you, boo boo.

Kelsey nods his head, patting Peyton on his back, like the gentleman he is. It appears all is forgiven between them, which makes me happy.

However, Peyton glares at me as if I were some murderous traitor that has committed the ultimate betrayal. He's exasperated. But he has not forgotten that the two us don't play on the same team here.

I give him a flirty wink hoping to soothe his angst.

"I say we move these negotiations along. Those shots are starting to sound like a good idea," I murmur.

"Shots were always a good idea, Paige. Right, baby?" Lexi says, directing her comment at Kelsey.

"Shots are a good idea, honey, but I'm gonna need a few beer backs with them after today. Probably gonna need a designated driver," Kelsey huffs.

"Let's move this negotiation along so we can get to it then," Peyton says, much more composed.

"Mmm. I agree," I add casually.

Peyton squints, gritting his teeth at me like a junkyard dog hungry for his last meal and I'm the red meat.

An afternoon with all this Peyton-ness is making me horny. Deep down I had no doubt he loved a good challenge, and today I've managed to bring it to him. The mere thought of besting him was practically orgasmic. I pushed my thighs together at the thought of it.

"I'm sure we can work our differences out," Peyton mutters.

My eyes widen with curiosity.

"Really? Okay. Whatcha got?"

CHAPTER TWO

I hate the fact that Paige has wielded the upper hand. Two hours of negotiation in, she was supposed to be on my turf, not the other way around. I'm losing. I had taken that course "Getting to Yes" in law school years ago, and hours later all I'm getting is a bunch of nos. My law school professors would be ashamed. My Harvard law education looks like it wasn't worth the sheepskin it was written on with all the abuse I'm taking at the hands of Paige. She is repping Penn Law school well. They say there is nothing better than a Philadelphia lawyer, and Paige is making me out to be a believer. When had she become this lethal? She is tearing me a new ass, all while making my dick hard.

Kelsey is sulking that I haven't brought closure to these negotiations because he's ready for those shots. And Lexi she's—Lexi. She couldn't care less about any of this. She trusts Paige to represent her best interests. She is blowing kisses at Kelsey every time a red line is drawn though his own Goddamn demands all while pledging her undying love for him. Kelsey just eats it up. He has officially surrendered his balls over to Lexi's gold-plated va-jay-jay. He has lost his right mind, forgetting that he and I are supposed to be a team. Kelsey, a managing partner in a world-class law firm, is letting Lexi kidnap his balls, holding them hostage, while Paige castrates him. I'm certain I am in the conference room with Lorena Bobbitt and her evil twin.

I place my hand on my own balls making sure mine are still in place. There is no fucking way I'm going to forget this day. This is exactly why I practice white collar crime staying out of matters related to contract law. Too much fucking emotion getting in my line of fire. No more favors for Kelsey going forward. He begged me for weeks to represent him. I pushed back telling him it was a bad idea. He needed an attorney that specialized in contract law. One who wasn't emotionally involved. I am his brother, for Christ's sake. I'm emotionally involved in so many ways I can't even begin to count. I'm to be best man at his wedding. And it isn't lost on him or Lexi that my heart beats to the rhythm of the queen of hearts sitting across the conference room table.

I tap my Montblanc pen on the table like a drummer on a snare, shaking my head every time Paige draws a red line across the page. Surely love is blind in one eye and can't see out the other at this table. Team Lexi is ahead ten to Team Kelsey's five. But I draw the line at Kelsey giving in to the demands that in the event of divorce, Lexi would take part ownership of Kelsey's shares in the Morrone Group. Lady Justice was going to have to lift her blindfold up long enough to keep one good eye open because like me, Kelsey owns a significant share of Morrone stock. If he put his dick in the wrong place down the road as some big shot Senator, there was no way the firm was going to be collateral damage beholden to Lexi Wang. No. Fucking. Way.

"Let it go, honey. You know you don't need my money," Kelsey says to Lexi at the thought of one more change.

There are so many red lines on the page the prenup looks like it's bleeding. He's right. He must have been reading my thoughts. Team Kelsey has promised Lexi a boatload of money in the event of divorce. Kelsey's property in the Hamptons, his summer home in St. Barts, year-round staff were all on the table. Paige even knocked the couple's future baby count down from four kids to two. *What's wrong with more babies?*

Lexi was given an unlimited line of credit on Kelsey's American Express black card, which made no sense because she has a boatload of cash and her own black card. She didn't need Kelsey's money. But apparently principles be damned when it came to babies. *Did I not say Lexi had more money than sense?*

Hell, if the tables were turned, the thought of being the man to make babies with Paige made my heart thump. I would use every chance I could get to make plenty of brown babies with her beautiful ass. I'd let that petite curvaceous body ride my dick until I made my own basketball team. Five boys with a beautiful brown baby sister as their coach. A baby girl that would grow up to look exactly like Paige. Even now as I stare across the table at her I could see my vision in the making. Paige has big curious hazel eyes with flecks of gold. Wavy chestnut brown locks that part on the side and fall over the side of her face and neck like a cascading waterfall. She has kissable lips that are tinted with a deep red lip gloss I'm dying to taste. I want nothing more than to run my hands across her smooth caramel-colored skin, branding her body with a spattering of kisses from her head to toes, my lips landing on her sweet spot to claim it as mine.

"Stop staring at me like that, Peyton. We're done here. Have Kelsey initial the changes. I'll forward a final copy to your office for signature," Paige says, startling me out of my daydream while sliding the marked-up prenup pages across the table. *God, this woman makes me nuts.*

I shake off my wayward thoughts that are betraying me. My dick is hard from thinking about making babies with Paige. I'm pretty sure I momentarily lost control of my senses and growled out loud. *Did I?*

"Pump your brakes, counselor. Now it's my turn to go take a piss," I snap back at her.

I rise from my chair, sliding the paperwork angrily at Kelsey's direction. I'm emotionally fed up in this sea of surrender. He is fully capable of putting his own neck in a noose of his making. He knows the game and the rules. Me, I was a fool to dabble in this business of prenuptial agreements because Kelsey is my younger brother. I should have stayed in my lane. White collar crime. That, I am good at. Good enough to catch criminals in the making like Paige. What she has accomplished with these prenuptial negotiations is a downright dirty crime. Fucking reprehensible. Ferociousness runs in my DNA, yet she's whipped me like one of the bad guys in those ninja turtles cartoons my nephew watches on Saturday mornings.

I stalk toward the exit, closing the conference room door behind me, determined to catch a much needed breath of fresh air. I need to collect my thoughts. The battle may have been lost, but I have no intentions of losing the war going on in my head and my heart. I have plans for Paige. We both knew Kelsey is so much in love that he would have laid the world at Lexi's feet at any cost. This negotiation was going to be a slam dunk for Paige no matter what. I knew that. Paige knew that. But still, I am determined to bring that sexy vixen down. Preferably down on top of me.

I head down the long hallway well past the men's bathroom and into the Top of the Thirty Club. I enter the restaurant, swiping my gold keycard against the card reader and nodding my head at the club concierge who is acknowledging me.

"Good evening, Mr. Morrone, Would you like your usual table?"

"Not today, Jacob. Are they still here?"

"Yes, Sir. Shall I escort you?"

"That won't be necessary. I see them."

Jacob nods at me, holding his hand outward to direct me towards their table.

I walk in in a semi-circle across the restaurant floor that is rotating in slow motion giving the guests a panoramic view of the city. I approach the silver-haired gentleman who is clutching the hand of the beautiful old lady. She has that familiar gleam in her eye holding on to his every word as if his mouth were a bible and he were spewing the gospel. She's totally enamored with the old man. He sees me out of the corner of his eye, and rises from the booth in greeting.

"Peyton, I was hoping you would grace us with your presence."

I shake his hand, then bend low to kiss her wrinkled cheek.

"Delilah, how many times have I told you to drop this old fool and ride off into the sunset. Just you and me, beautiful."

She laughs at me with loving wrinkled eyes and pats my hand, coaxing me to sit next to her.

"I can't stay long," I say, as I take a seat.

She pats me on my forearm with affection.

"I've missed talking to you, sweet boy. Of all my grand-children, Peyton, you are my favorite."

I entangle my fingers in between hers as my grandfather snorts.

"Mother, you tell that to all the grands. Besides, Peyton, haven't you heard? Three's a crowd."

I laugh out loud at him.

"I see he's still full of jokes this afternoon, Delilah."

My grandmother demanded that her grandkids call her by her first name. She felt the term *grandmother* made her seem old. She was not going to surrender to the idea of old age in this lifetime ever. She was the youngest seventy year old that I knew. Grandfather didn't care what he was called as long as he was both seen and heard.

"Last I checked, Grandfather, your middle name could be threesome," I quip back at him with a wink. "I know you love company."

"You don't meet the qualifications, my boy," Grandfather laughs, followed by his signature wink.

Grandmother pats my hand.

"He can barely handle me, let alone anyone else. Why do you think he's been so faithful all these years? Oh, the games the man can play."

"Doesn't mean a man can't dream, Mother. I'm not dead yet."

"You sound like a creepy old man, William. Truth is, you love the attention of others," she says full of sass.

"Can't say you don't know me, woman," Grandfather answers back.

The waiter drops a sherry on the table for my grandmother and two whiskeys for me and Grandfather. Regular membership has its privileges. The servers know our drinks.

Grandfather thanks the server with a nod.

"No really, I can't stay long. Ms. Holland is beating the pants off me in a prenuptial negotiation. We're in the main conference room down the hall. I only stopped in here to make sure my balls were still attached to the rest of my body. That's how bad it's been going."

"She's Ms. Holland now? That beauty must be whipping the pants off you. If only I could be a fly on the wall. She's the only person I know that can drive you off your game. Or shall I say beating you at your own game."

Grandfather chuckles before taking a gulp of his whiskey.

"She thinks I've gone to the men's room. But I needed to toss back a whiskey with my favorite couple to collect my bearings."

"See, boy, I knew threesomes were in your DNA," Grandfather says with a laugh. "What do you young folk call it now? We're having a whiskey throuple."

"Peyton, ignore your grandfather. He rode up the elevator today with Paige. They pretended they didn't know each other. He even invited her to join us for dinner. She went along with his game, turning him down, of course. Those two like role playing more than anyone I know."

Role Playing, there's a thought. I could imagine role playing with Paige. Her on her knees, me with a fist full of her hair in hand and her lips moaning against my dick.

"She stayed in character and acted like she had no idea who I was," Delilah chuckles. "I'm starting to raise an eyebrow with both of them. Your grandfather is starting to attract recruits into his little theatrics. I hope you're keeping that beautiful lady happy."

"He's boring her to tears," Grandfather teases. "She could use a touch of excitement in her life."

I take a huge swig of my whiskey, downing it in one gulp. Grandfather is trying to get my goat. He testing my armor to make sure I have no room for insecurity when it comes to Paige. He loves her almost as much as I do, and she him.

"Stick to exciting your own woman, old man. You leave Ms. Holland to me."

I bend close to kiss my grandmother on her cheek.

"I've gotta run, Delilah. Time for me to show that pretty young thing who's boss."

Grandmother practically falls out of her chair with laughter. I stand to leave, patting Grandfather on his shoulder affectionately.

"Good luck. We'll be right here having dessert if you're at risk for losing your junk again, son."

I fought an eye roll, hearing his laughter in the background as I leave the club. Grandfather can practically smell the scent of loser on me. He knows Paige has gotten the best of me today. He knows that losing is not an emotion I know how to wear well.

I arrive back in the conference room at the same time Paige is stuffing the contract documents in her bag. Kelsey and Lexi are across the room holding hands exchanging small talk in between their kisses.

"So you finally decided to grace us with your presence again, Mr. Morrone?

"I couldn't stand the thought of being away from you too long. I figure I should stick around long enough for a bit of your charms to rub off on me. No one can ever say you're not good at what you do, Paige."

She gives me a bewildering smile.

"I like to think that's more skill than charm. Besides, I had a good teacher."

"Perhaps there are things you could teach me. I've been known to be a good student."

I sing the first few bars of Al Jarreau's "Teach Me Tonight." She giggles. I love the cute sound she makes. Her eyes twinkle, enjoying my renewed sense of humor and playfulness.

"Hey, Peyton," Kelsey interrupts our exchange. "Lexi and I decided we're going to forego any business of stock exchanges. We're never going to divorce. We're in it for the long haul. Isn't that right, baby?" Kelsey adds with an air of pride.

"Yeah. Let's go party on and celebrate," Lexi says. "We're overdue for those shots."

I rub my hand across the top of my brow from emotional fatigue. I've had enough of the Kelsey-Lexi dog and pony show for one day. It's time for me to extract myself from this situation. Paige is ignoring them too and is back to packing up her belongings. She knows her work here is done. Mine is too, but my work with her is far from done.

I glance at my watch, grabbing my phone and opening up my calendar before tapping my fingers across the keyboard on my phone.

"So what's it going to be, Peyton? You twisted my arm earlier to agree to go do shots. You owe me a few rounds by my calculations."

I decide to make up an excuse so as to launch my own extraction plan. I glance down at my phone that's buzzing on the conference room table. I swipe it open, reading a text message from Jackie.

"Sorry guys. I'll have to take a rain check on those shots. Jackie just reminded me that I have a late-night plane to catch. I need to head downstairs to the office and take care of some last-minute matters before I leave town."

"Jackie?" Kelsey responds. "We gave the entire office the

afternoon off, remember? Your workaholic tendencies need curbing. Poor Jackie can't catch a break working for you."

"Vegas calls. Besides, Kelsey, some of us have to stay focused on the bottom line. Some of us might try to give away the shop in the name of love," I add with a raised eyebrow.

Paige lifts her head from her phone, narrowing her eyes at me, pleading silently with me to play nice. *Okay. So that was a low blow.* But fuck it. Paige had dug deep in her bag of wicked tricks today. *Color me salty.* Still, I wave my hand at Kelsey dismissively. Lexi shrugs her shoulders as if she couldn't care less whether I go or not. She's got what she wanted today with Paige's help, so now her priorities have changed.

"Sorry, Paige. Maybe we can meet up for drinks another time. A rain check perhaps?"

She gives me a disappointed stare.

"No worries, Peyton. I'm a big girl. Black girl magic knows how to change lanes," she coos seductively.

It genuinely hurts me to reject her, but I have a more important mission. Today is an important day. Not a day that I can fuck around. But still, I can't ignore the wildness in her eyes daring to break free. She looks genuinely fuckable. Her look of repressed desire makes the hardness in my pants grow.

"C'mon, Paige, let's go throw back those shots," Lexi says, rolling her eyes at me. "If Peyton wants to poop out on our celebration, let him. This is not the time to pull that over-sized stick out of his ass."

Touché, Lexi. I was owed that slam. Now I have complete confidence that my future nieces and nephews won't be bullied in the world. Momma's got a spine.

Lexi grabs Paige's hand nudging her towards the door.

Paige follows behind with an air of reluctance, her steps much slower. I take that as a sign.

So I decide to commit to my plans. I'm no longer in the mood to share Paige's attention with Kelsey and Lexi in a crowded bar tonight. I'd much rather have her all to myself.

CHAPTER THREE

P addy's is packed with a huge March Madness and St. Patrick's Day crowd. Lucky for us, Kelsey has a table reserved on the upper deck in the VIP section when we arrive. VIP status has its perks when you find your-self in the middle of a sports bar. The basketball games are playing on all the televisions in the restaurant. Champagne, tumblers, and shot glasses filled with green drinks are being sloshed around as the servers move through the crowd with trays of entrees, appetizers and alcohol. The noise level is loud from the broadcasters and the patrons' raucous shouting and fist bumping every time their team makes a basket. Green and gold beads hang on most of the reveler's necks. Some are sporting glittering green glasses on their faces, and the Luck of the Irish top hats on their heads. Villanova was in the hunt with Penn, and fans of both teams were chasing the win. Even though I have a dog in the fight—go Penn!—I focus on the menu. I order oysters on the half shell, lobster rolls, fries and margaritas for me and Lexi. Our version of comfort food. Kelsey, sitting in the booth between me and Lexi, orders a bottle of Johnnie Walker Blue Label, hot wings and jalapeño cornbread. He is more focused on the game than us. Kelsey's team makes a three pointer at the quarter buzzer, and he pulls Lexi under his arm kissing her temple. He's happily in love, and she is as well. Kelsey's display of affection for Lexi makes me think about my own person. It also makes me think more deeply about my day with Peyton. He is a quick-witted, handsome, sexy and powerful man. Being in his orbit brings butterflies to my stomach. I get goosebumps thinking of him. Getting the most out of today's negotiation for Lexi filled me with excitement and joy. I had gotten the win I set out to achieve, but he wasn't the kind of man a smart woman should ignore.

I ran my tongue across the salt rim of my margarita, licking my lips and thinking about my own tall, handsome and enigmatic man. A man who must have been reading my mind because my phone buzzes as my thoughts veer to him.

SHAKER: Hey baby.

MOVER: Hey boo.

SHAKER: Are you somewhere where you need to be or want to be?

MOVER: I'm not where I want to be or need to be.

SHAKER: I know how to get you to where you need to be.

MOVER: Which is where?

SHAKER: In my arms of course.

MOVER: Do you have plans for me still?

SHAKER: Yes. But first, you need to atone.

MOVER: Really? For what?

SHAKER: You're late. Again. You know I don't like to be kept waiting.

MOVER: It's been that kind of day.

SHAKER: You're stress smoking again. I found your cigarettes.

Omg, he found my cigarettes. Damn, I was careless. I didn't want him to know all my tells, and stress smoking was one of them.

MOVER: What can I say? You drive me crazy big dog. *☺*

SHAKER: So now your kitty cat has to pay for your bad deeds. The price of atonement. You're in trouble. *☺ *

MOVER: Nothing like good trouble.

SHAKER: Trouble is my middle name. *☺ *I'm on to you. And, I'm coming for you.

I swipe my phone closed, tossing it in my purse. I scan the restaurant. I'm certain he has eyes on me. I don't see him, but I sense him. I know he's here. I peer over the balcony of the second floor, glancing down to the first floor. I search for his tall figure amongst the crowd of rebel rousers raising glasses to their team.

The server arrives with our oysters. I squeeze a slice of lemon across one of them, the seeds falling on the side of the plate as I suck an oyster down my throat. I wipe my mouth with the back of my hand, hoping he's watching me suck down his favorite aphrodisiac. I slide out of the circular booth leaving Lexi and Kelsey to themselves.

"I'm going to the ladies' room." I grab my small silver micro clutch out of the inside pocket of my tote, tucking my phone inside it, and stuffing my suit and trench coat inside the larger bag. I open the tiny silver clutch, slipping the sparkly five-caret pink diamond onto my tan-lined ring finger.

"Watch my things for me, Lexi?"

She nods with a raised eyebrow as she catches me slipping my ring on. She doesn't say a word, but goes back to the mindless conversation with Kelsey.

I amble down the winding staircase to the first floor. I move through the crowd, bumping shoulders with people crowding the long bar in the main room watching the game. I weave in between them and across the shiny hardwood floors, like a beacon traveling through a maze, destined to land on its honing device. I walk down a long hallway leading past the private banquet rooms near the ladies' restroom. I'm momentarily disappointed that I don't see him. This is not my imagination. I know he's here. And then I hear our song. Marvin Gaye's "After the Dance" is playing. I follow the sound of the music. It's coming from a private party room that the restaurant typically reserves for special events. I step inside the room that appears to have a wedding reception underway. The party is in full blast. I still have on my work clothes, my navy pin-striped pencil skirt and black patent Louboutin's. Thank god, attire wise, I fit in. I unbutton a couple of the pearl buttons on my silk silver blouse. I weave through the crowd, crossing the dance floor, ignoring the bodies swaying in time with each other. I grab a glass of champagne off the tray of one of the servers. I gulp it down, then set the empty glass and my clutch in front of an empty chair next to a couple of guests who are headed to the dance floor. I give them a pleasant smile.

"Great party, right?" I say to the woman who's headed to the dance floor.

"So much fun," she answers back with a wide grin.

I stay on the move, pushing through the crowd, searching for him. No one realizes I'm a party crasher. I move in a circle to the other side of the room, still searching. I'm buzzed from margaritas and the champagne chaser, but my senses are still on high alert. I run my hands down the sides of my navy blue pencil skirt shimmying my hips in place on the edge of the dance floor. I start to sway my body side to side with the beating music. Two big strong hands grasp both sides of my hips from behind me. A crackled thunderbolt of current passes between us. I grab on to his hands as we sway to the beat of the music, his tall frame towering over me. I press my back against his chest. His thick bulge grinds against my ass. He bends his head low, his hot breath and lips pressing against my ear.

"I hear you're a troublemaker, lady. Are the rumors true?" His whispered voice is deep and sexy in my ear.

I smile, my eyes close as he sways his hard body against my back moving us to the beat of the music.

"I could say that about you. You're the party crasher," I hum, melting into his arms.

"Woman, I am the party," he says.

"I love parties."

"I'm not fond of parties where every man in here has their eyes on you. I may need to bust some balls. These men think they can have what's mine."

"I'm a big girl. I can take care of myself. So little trust."

"It's not you I'm worried about," he growls in my ear. "Why do you think they call me the Shaker?"

"Ah let me guess. Because you get off on shaking things up," I giggle.

"Yes. And that goes for every man in here who's hot on your trail."

"You're such the force to be reckoned with, my sweet. I see the green-eyed devil is riding your shoulder again."

"Well you best move him off, baby."

We laugh together, lost in our private moment of wonderment.

He spins me around, his seductive glare burning a hole in

my soul. His body keeping beat to the tempo of the music. He pulls me in close. My man can dance. He slides his hands down my ass, palming my butt. I gasp a breath of air. He squeezes me tighter pulling me into his chest. He kisses me on the lips, catching me off guard. My head floats under the weight of his touch. Although he's not normally the PDA type, he is tonight.

"Now they know for sure you're mine. They want what I have."

He gives me a torturous wink. I melt in his arms as the lust between us builds. He spins me around, out and then back close in his arms.

"Can I have you, Paige?" he whispers in my ear.

He runs his tongue down my ear lobe, poking his tongue in my ear.

"Look at you," I chuckle with delight. "Asking for permission. I believe I heard somewhere on the grapevine you were a chivalrous man."

"Who said I was chivalrous? Liars. The whole damn grapevine."

He gives me a wolfish smirk. He swings me out wide, twirling me around in a circle then swinging me back into his arms. His free hand sweeps a stray lock of hair from his face.

My lungs rummage for air. A jolt of electricity thunderbolts between us again.

"And why should I let you have me?" I tease, wrapping both my arms up high around the nape of his neck. I thread my fingers through the back of his hair, catching a swatch of his hair, pulling him closer.

He presses me against his hard rod, whispering sweet sexy words in my ear.

"Atonement, darlin'. I need those red-bottom heels

wrapped around my ears, baby," he whispers, making a throaty groan in my ear.

"Permission granted."

I stare into his heated gaze, licking my lips as we sway together, his moves a dance of seduction. My panties are wet. It's taking everything I have to hold on to the little semblance of sanity I have left. His intensity is driving me crazy. It's mind-blowing.

The music changes to another song, and some of the coupled dancers leave the dance floor as new ones join the dance floor.

"Come, Paige. It's time for us to get on the move."

I'm certain he's short-circuited my brain as he pulls me out of my lust-filled haze.

He places his hand on the small of my back guiding me through the crowd. He stops at the cash bar, pays for a shot of Jack Daniels, and swigs it down, while I text Lexi to tell her I'm leaving and to grab my things. She texts me smiley faces and heart emojis back. I grin believing my bestie and I are the luckiest gals in the world. We both have our persons. We both are in love.

He grabs my hand, fingering my ring first, then weaving us through a crowd of revelers and out the door of the restaurant. A white stretch limousine is waiting. The driver standing at the ready. He opens our door with his familiar smile.

"Ma'am," the driver says.

I nod, glad to see him.

"Sir." He tips his hat at him.

I have no idea where we are going nor do I care at this

moment. Wherever he is going, I am following him like the fool in love that I am.

I slide across the leather seat first, and he climbs in behind me. Pushing the button he closes the partition off from us and our driver. He pours two snifters of whiskey, handing me a tumbler swirling with amber liquid. He takes a gulp of the hot liquid, then kisses me with a mouth full of whiskey, transferring it into my mouth. I swallow, my chest heating as he teases me with hungry eyes. He rakes his hand slowly from my ankle up to my thigh finding his way under the hem of my skirt. He's back to seducing me, picking up from where we left off on the dance floor. He wants to play.

"How was your day?" I ask, licking my tongue around the rim of the glass. My insides are warming but I can't decide if it's the whiskey or him.

"It was interesting. Friends. Family. War."

He gives me a smug smile, his hand reaching the edge of my soaked panties.

"How was yours? Kill anybody today?

He raises his eyebrow curiously, his lips dragging across my own as his fingers reach my center. My thoughts rewind back to my skilled negotiations with that alpha dog, Peyton Morrone.

"It was interesting. Friends. Family. War."

I set my glass down in the cup holder next to his. My mind clouds as he inserts two fingers inside me, the wetness coating them. I moan as he inserts those fingers in my mouth after tasting them himself first. He unbuttons my blouse, lowering his head and swirling his tongue underneath my black lace bra, finding the hardened nipple of my breast. He gives my nipple a tug with his teeth. He is back to fingering me. My breathing picks up as I chase my orgasm. He slides my skirt up to my waist, pulling my panties down and off. He sniffs them. He places them in the pocket of his neatly pressed pants.

"You dirty boy," I moan on the brink of combustion, shivers crawling up my spine.

"You like me dirty," he says, lying me backwards, spreading my legs apart, then running his tongue down my landing strip. He plunges his tongue inside me.

He bends low towards me, raising my red-bottom-heeled legs on each side of his ears. Just like he promised. I'm spread eagle, my legs wrapped around his head.

" You…you...you..."

I moan breathily unable to form a complete sentence on the brink of another climax.

"Use your words, Paige," he says kissing my sex in between licks, his breath a caress.

"Ahh...You feel so good."

I try to sneak a hand between us, to reach down in his pants to feel the one thing I need. He grabs my wrists, stopping me, shoving his tongue in my mouth for a dirty boy kiss. I work hard to grab his penis. I need to feel him inside me.

"No, no, no, baby. You're atoning. You have to wait a bit longer to get to this," he chuckles.

"You're punishing me," I answer breathily.

"In the worst kind of way, my love. Trust me, it's hurting me more than it ever could hurt you. But we need to change our mode of transportation right now."

"You can't leave me like this. Wanting. In need."

He reaches over and kisses me again on the lips, his eyes raking over my body like a hungry lion that has laid in wait on his prey.

"Patience, sweetheart. I'm far from done with you yet."

The limousine comes to a quick halt. He lifts his two-hundred pounds off me. He pulls my skirt down over my hips, smoothing it out, pulling me back up to a seating position. I know without looking at myself that I have that "just fucked" look on my face. He drinks a swig of his whiskey and I do the same. I sweep my hair off my face, grab my silver clutch and retouch my lipstick gloss, patting my hair down as best I could. I don't know where we're headed next.

"We have company," he says, reading my thoughts, looking his composed and stoic, self-assured self. My mysterious man is changing gears.

The limousine stops, and the driver opens the door. We're at the airstrip. I see the family private jet on the runway. *The Legal Eagle.* It's all coming together. He steps out of the limousine extending his hand to help me out. He rests his palm on the small of my back, guiding me towards our private plane. We walk up the stairs to the plane where our pilot, Wesley, is waiting to greet us.

"Mr. Morrone, Mrs. Morrone, so good to see you again."

"Hey, Wesley," Peyton grins at him.

"Paige, so glad to have you on board again today," our uniformed flight attendant says cheerily. "Peyton. Good to see you, Sir. Your family is already on board and seated."

Family on board? Once again, Peyton is full of surprises.

"We've logged in the flight plan to Las Vegas, Sir," Wesley says to Peyton. "We'll be taking off in about fifteen minutes upon clearance."

"Are my grandparents on board?"

"They are, sir. Your brother and his fiancé are here too."

"Great," Peyton answers. "Let's get this party underway. I've got plans for my wife this weekend."

"Well, you were late tonight, Sir. I had to change my flight plan once more."

"Yeah, Wes, I know. Late should be my wife's middle name. We should all learn to adjust our watches and time zones for Paige Holland Morrone."

I huff at the both of them, rolling my eyes as Wes and Peyton laugh and high five.

I stroll to the back of the cabin with Peyton on my heels.

Lexi, Kelsey, Delilah, and Peyton's grandfather, William, are in their seats. My favorite couples. Lexi and Kelsey are chit-chatting with each other. William and Delilah are playing a game of chess on a mini chessboard.

Everyone turns their attention towards Peyton and me. They yell out in unison, "Surprise! Happy Anniversary!"

Peyton bends down whispering in my ear.

"Happy Anniversary, baby. I told you I had something special planned for you tonight."

I hold back happy tears. I glance at Peyton's grandfather, William Morrone, who's wearing a Cheshire cat smile on his face. That old man is full of surprises. I have no doubt that Peyton is working hard to keep his grandfather's legacy of fun and games going.

William gets up from his seat, placing his body in front of me with Peyton in the aisle, behind me, and I'm in the middle.

"Did I tell you how much I love threesomes?" he says, taking my hands in his.

"I believe you did, William. Today in the elevator."

I raise a crooked eyebrow at him and laugh.

"You're the best thing that ever happen to my grandson. Happy anniversary, sweetheart."

William kisses me on the cheek softly.

"Keep away, old man," Peyton teases. We all laugh.

"Thank you, Grandpa William," I say, kissing him back. "You really had me fooled this time in the elevator."

"And you, my dear, are a great mark," he laughs heartily.

"Sit down, William," Delilah instructs him. "You can't keep recruiting Peyton's wife into your shenanigans. And Paige is not a mark. You're more likely the mark."

Everyone laughs.

"Peyton should thank me," William says, moving back to his seat next to Delilah. "Paige wears the look of a woman that has had some real excitement in her day."

"I can't argue with that," I laugh out loud.

"A win against Peyton. A threesome proposition. An atonement. Doesn't get any better than that," I say, knowing that only Peyton and I get my private joke about atonement.

"Mission accomplished, Grandfather. But now I need a private one-on-one conference with my wife. Come, Paige."

Peyton grabs my hand scurrying me to the private room in the back of our plane. *The bedroom.*

"Your turn at surrendering today, baby," my husband whispers in my ear so no one can hear.

Heat coils in my stomach that is filled with flutters again.

"You know, Paige, the tables have turned. You beat me today in the conference room," he says with an intense look in his eye.

"I was ready for you this time," I smile, mesmerized by his smoldering gaze. "You taught me well, Peyton."

"Well, when the student is ready, the teacher appears."

Peyton flashes his wolfish smirk.

"Whatcha got, Paige?"

I place a soft kiss on his lips and close the door behind us.

The End.

AUTHOR NOTES

I hope you enjoyed Peyton and Paige. I penned this short novella to share my stories with you in hopes that you'll want to read more of my novels in the multicultural romantic suspense genre. My stories typically feature female heroines with wealthy alpha males on their heels for love. In these novels, you'll find exciting, steamy, twists and turns with smoking hot alpha males. Like me, you're welcome to adopt those hotties as your own personal book boyfriends. What's not to fall in love about them?

If you delighted in Peyton and Paige's story, I invite you to explore my other stand-alone multicultural romantic suspense novels featured on both my website and Amazon pages. Flip the page to find out how to hunt those hot honey's down.

XOXO
Jude E. McNamara

A Word About the Author

I am Jude E. McNamara. Virtual adventurer. Keyboard ninja. Guardian of sassy romantic encounters. I am the alter ego of that other woman, Jude. You know, the one that loves snowy nights, is in a relationship with love, and looking for her own hero. While by day she's off being the disciplined scrappy businesswoman with the mind of a shark, I gallivant her keyboard by night, running wild and free on the downlow. I figure she'll have to catch up to me. Because once that blue power button turns on, I'm far too busy breathing life into those colorful characters that run around in her head, incessantly telling me their stories even if it's at the break of dawn.

You can find me and my merry band of jet-setting girlfriends running from the paparazzi at the high-end cocktail bars in Manhattan, drinking Patron Silver. I'm the flashy one wearing the sparkly tiara on my head. Like clockwork, when she faithfully dons her track shoes to catch up with me, I usually have to listen to her lecture me about my behavior over a glass of champagne. She loves champagne. Actually I love champagne too—except I like mine with a side of tall, handsome hunk begging me to stop at the intersection of heartbreak hotel and romantic encounter road, demanding a happily ever after.

It's an arduous race to "The End" before her blue button

goes dark and I cease to exist. But once the blue light appears, the race is on, right up to the point when we two Judes meet on the same page, often in a book like this one.

For more about the author, visit: www.judeemcnamara.com
Two Judes Publishing.com

facebook.com/JudeE.McNamara

twitter.com/@judeemcnamara

instagram.com/iamtwojudes

amazon.com/author/judeemcnamara

ALSO BY JUDE E. MCNAMARA

WINGMAN (A BLACK SEQUINNED BOWS AND CHAMPAGNE NIGHTS PREQUEL NOVELLA.)

Love and loyalty are powerful forces. Love compelled my need to get in the game. Love beckoned me on a path to catch the curveball headed my way.

BLACK SEQUINNED BOWS AND CHAMPAGNE NIGHTS.

What's a woman to do when a sexy Navy Captain steps into her life as tragedy strikes, and a secret is revealed. Can newfound love survive the discovery?

MILK MONEY

New York's Angel Investor extraordinaire has the perfect life of wealth, power, and prestige. Almost. Gone is the missing long-time love of his life.

SUGAR MOMMY ON TOP

Will the man who spends his days and nights bringing new life into the world be able to heal himself while mending her broken heart, igniting an unexpected flame of love between them?

CHASING WINTER

Once upon a time we were the halves to each other's hearts. Still, I left a trail of broken hearts in my wake—both hers and mine. Seven years later, I'm coming back for what was once mine–her. I will do whatever it takes. Once upon a time, she danced to the beat of my heart. Now she dances to the beat of her own drum.

STAY CONNECTED WITH JUDE

Thank you again for your readership and support. If you enjoyed this book, please leave a review at your favorite book retailer and Goodreads. If you would like to learn about my other books, you may wish to sign up for my newsletter to be notified when my new novels are released.

Visit me online at judeemcnamara.com where you can learn more about me, find book trailers, my blog posts and other new upcoming work.

Best Regards

Jude E. McNamara
https://www.judeemcnamara.com
Email Jude: jude@judeemcnamara.com
Subscribe to my newsletter: judeemcnamara.com/contact-jude

Follow me on Twitter @judeemcnamara
Follow me on Instagram: iamtwojudes

Follow me on Facebook: Jude E. McNamara
Visit me on Goodreads: Jude E. McNamara